BILL'S
NEW
FROCK

Anne Fine

HIT PLAYS

THE FWOG PWINCE by Kaye Umansky
BELIEVE IN THE STARS by Gaylord Meech
BILL'S NEW FROCK by Anne Fine
THE COMPUTER NUT by Betsy Byars
COLLISION COURSE by Nigel Hinton
MAID MARIAN AND HER MERRY MEN
   by Tony Robinson

HIT BOOKS

EVA by Peter Dickinson
ACROSS THE FRONTIER
   by Christine Pullein-Thompson
THE LANDFILL by David Leney
CHINA LEE by Sue Limb
HI THERE, SUPERMOUSE! by Jean Ure
NICOLA MIMOSA by Jean Ure
THE TRICKSTERS by Margaret Mahy
THE COACHMAN RAT by David Henry Wilson
TWISTERS stories from other centuries

Series Editors

Robin Little
Patrick Redsell
Erik Wilcock

CONTENTS

This play was first broadcast on BBC Radio 5 in 1990. It was produced by Peter Hutchings and dramatised by Richard Pinner.

Introduction

Bill's New Frock was first performed on radio in an adaptation by Richard Pinner from Anne Fine's original story. It is now one of the books in the series, **Hit Plays**, all of which have been produced either for television or radio.

The plays in the series are for readers aged 11–13. This does not mean that all of them are the same in any way; they are as varied as the people who will study them as part of their reading programme for Key Stage 3 in English. The one thing the plays have in common is that they are enjoyable to read.

On the next page you will find a section entitled 'What the play is about'. This summarises the action in the play as well as focusing on some of the main issues dealt with in it. Following this, there is a section called 'Preparing for reading'. This gives the information you need to read the play successfully. There are brief descriptions of the characters, who they are and how much they have to say.

At the end of the book there are two sections which outline some activities you can do after you have read the play. 'Drama activities' (page 35) provides clearly organised ways of getting to grips with the script and how it works in production. 'Writing and talking about the play' (page 36) gives some straight-forward assignments to help you in your understanding of the play.

What the play is about

When Bill wakes up on Monday morning, he finds that somehow, in the night, he has turned into a girl. Even his mother, when she comes in the bedroom, suggests he wears a frilly pink frock to school. After she drops it over his head, nothing seems to be the same. Bella the cat doesn't notice any change, but everyone else treats him differently. An old lady wants to help him over the road. Mean Malcolm wolf-whistles him instead of kicking him. The headmaster calls him 'dear'. Mrs Collins expects neater work. And Bill, picked to read the part of Rapunzel, gets to see a fairy tale princess's life in a new light! His attempt to join in the football game as usual is a disaster, and he learns a bitter lesson about the need for pockets, even in frilly clothing.

Bill's dreadful day unfolds – one horror after another – emphasising in a thought-provoking and amusing way, just what it means to be treated as a girl rather than as a boy.

Preparing for reading

This play is written in very straightforward yet humorous language and should not present too many problems. There are thirty-one speaking parts: fifteen females and sixteen males.

The action of the play takes in two main locations: Bill's home and Bill's school, and covers a time span of one day. Since the play deals with events during a nightmarish school day, the language, ideas and humour should be easily recognisable to most pupils.

Character	Description	Role
BILL	school boy	large
MUM	Bill's mother	medium
DAD	Bill's father	small
BELLA	Bill's cat	small
OLD LADY	passer-by	small
MALCOLM	mean school boy	medium
HEADMASTER	Bill's Head	medium
BOY 1	school boy	small
BOY 2	school boy	small
BOY 3	school boy	small
MRS COLLINS	teacher	medium
ASTRID	school girl	medium
FLORA	school girl	small
KIRSTY	school girl	small
TALILAH	school girl	small
ROHAN	school boy	medium

Character	Description	Role
PHILIP	school boy	small
MARTIN	school boy	small
ARIF	school boy	small
NICK	school boy	small
MRS BANDA	teacher	medium
LEILA	school girl	medium
MELISSA	school girl	small
PAUL	school boy	small
WAYNE	school boy	small
NURSE	school nurse	small
JANITOR	school caretaker	small
SECRETARY	school secretary	small
LAURA	school girl	small
MARK	school boy	small

This play can easily be read around the class in a single session. It can also be read in groups of five or six. As long as the readers for Bill and the other main characters with medium-speaking parts remain constant, the others can negotiate the rest of the reading themselves on a scene-by-scene basis, doubling up parts where necessary. At the beginning of each scene, the characters who appear in it are listed.

To get you started

Before you start reading the play, here is an issue that you might like to discuss.

When someone says they have had a 'nightmare' of a day, what do they mean by this? Think of some things that might happen to you, which would make you consider them to be like a nightmare.

Bill's New Frock

Note: For the length of the play, nobody appears to notice any particular change in Bill. And throughout, whilst improvising, actors should be careful to avoid addressing him by name.

Scene 1: Bill's bedroom

(BILL, MUM, DAD, and BELLA the cat)

(*An alarm clock rings.*)

BILL
When I woke up that morning, something really strange had happened. Oh, my room looked exactly the same. And all the stuff in it looked exactly the same. Even the mirror looked exactly the same. But when I looked into the mirror, *I* didn't look exactly the same at all. I'd turned into a girl!

I don't believe this! Is it a *dream*? Is it a *nightmare*? What is going on?

MUM
(*calling*) Bill! Bill! Hurry up! Time to get dressed for school!

BILL
This can't be true. This can't be happening. I must still be asleep.

MUM
(*coming in*) Oh, good. You're awake.

BILL
That's that, then. I'm not asleep.

MUM
Up you get. Time to get dressed. Why don't you wear this pretty pink frock?

BILL
I never wear frocks!

MUM
I know. It's such a pity!

BILL
Don't drop that frock over my head! Mum, don't! Stop it! I can't breathe. (*gurgle, gurgle*) Mu-um!

3

MUM	There. Now it's on. I'll leave you to do up all the pretty little shell buttons. I'm late for work.
BILL	This can't be true. This simply cannot be true. Where's Dad? He'll sort me out. Dad! Dad!
DAD	Well, hello, poppet! You look very sweet today. It's not often we see you in a frock, is it?
BILL	Dad –
DAD	Take care now. I'm late for work.
BELLA	Miaowwwww. Miaowwwww.
BILL	Hello, Bella. At least you don't notice any difference in me, do you? I look the same to you. Oh, Bella! Is this a dream? Or a nightmare? Do I have to go to school like this?
BELLA	Miaowwwwww.
BILL	Yes. I suppose I do . . .

Scene 2: Outside the school

(BILL, HEADMASTER, BOYS 1, 2 and 3, OLD LADY and
MALCOLM)

OLD LADY	Give me your hand, dear. Let me help you safely across the road.
BILL	No thanks. Don't drag me. Let go.
OLD LADY	There we are. Safe and sound.
BILL	I've crossed here every day for months and she's never done that before. It must be this awful pink frock.
MALCOLM	(*wolf-whistling*) Wheeeet-whoooo!
BILL	It is! It's this awful pink frock! Even Mean Malcolm doesn't know who I am. He's wolf-whistling at me. Yuk! Uh-uh. There's the Headmaster, and I'm late. I'd better get through the gates.
HEADMASTER	(*yelling*) Come along, you lads! Get your skates on! Move, David Irwin! Hurry along, Tom Warren! Stop dawdling, Andrew!
BILL	I'll just try and creep past . . .
HEADMASTER	(*sweetly*) That's right, dear. Come along. We wouldn't like to be late for school now, would we?
BILL	Is he talking to *me*? He's never spoken to me like that before. It must be the frock. At least it keeps you out of trouble.

5

BOY 1	Hey, you!
BILL	Whoops! Maybe it doesn't.
BOY 1	Hey, you! Aren't you listening? Get out of the way of our football game.
BILL	Football! Oh, great! I'll be on your side. OK. Here we go. Ready. Kick it this way!
BOY 2	Get out of the way, can't you?
BILL	But I'm playing football with you.
BOY 3	No, you're not.
BOY 1	You can't. Not in that frock. No one plays football in a fancy frock like that!
BILL	I do.
BOY 2	Don't be silly. You're holding up our game. Get out of the way!
BOY 3	Go and play in the girls' bit of the playground.
BILL	Oh, yes? And where's that?
BOY 3	(*pointing one way*) Over there.
BILL	There are boys playing football over there.
BOY 2	(*pointing the other way*) Over there, then.
BILL	There are more boys playing football over there.
BOY 1	Over here, then.

BILL	You're playing here. You're playing everywhere.
BOY 3	It's not *our* problem, is it? Just get out of the way, please. You're spoiling the game.
BILL	No wonder most of the girls end up stuck against the railings if they're not playing football! There's nowhere else for them to go. If they come out into the middle of the playground, they'll get run over –
BOY 1 BOY 2 BOY 3	Get out of the way!
BILL	Just like I'm getting run over! Help! (*The bell rings. Everyone runs off, leaving Bill like an upturned crab in the middle of the playground.*)

Scene 3: Inside the classroom

(BILL, MRS COLLINS, HEADMASTER, ASTRID, FLORA, KIRSTY, ALL
THE GIRLS, ROHAN, PHILIP, MARTIN, ARIF and the WHOLE
CLASS)

MRS COLLINS	Good morning, everybody.
WHOLE CLASS	Good-mor-ning-Mis-sus-Col-lins.
MRS COLLINS	And here's the Headteacher to speak to you.
HEADMASTER	Good morning, 4C.
WHOLE CLASS	Good-mor-ning-Mis-ter-Phil-lips.
HEADMASTER	Now I want four strong volunteers to carry tables over to the playground for me.
ASTRID	Me, Sir!
BILL	Me, Sir!
KIRSTY	Me, Sir!
ROHAN	Me, Sir!
WHOLE CLASS	Me, Sir! I'm strong!
HEADMASTER	Right. This boy.
ROHAN	Yes, Sir.
HEADMASTER	And that boy.
MARTIN	Yes, Sir.
HEADMASTER	And that boy.
PHILIP	Yes, Sir.
HEADMASTER	And this boy.

8

ARIF	Yes, Sir.
HEADMASTER	Right. Off we go.
	(*Four boys and Headmaster troop out.*)
ASTRID	It's not fair, Mrs Collins.
FLORA	He always picks the boys to carry things.
MRS COLLINS	Perhaps the tables are heavy.
KIRSTY	None of the tables in this school are heavy.
ASTRID	And I know for a fact that I am stronger than at least three of the boys he picked.
BILL	It's true. Whenever we have a tug of war, everyone wants Astrid on their team.
MRS COLLINS	Oh, well. It doesn't matter. No need to make such a fuss. It's only a silly old table.
ALL THE GIRLS	But it *does* matter. To *us*.
MRS COLLINS	That's enough! Now everyone open your workbooks.
WHOLE CLASS	. . . mutter . . . mutter . . . mutter . . .
MRS COLLINS	And get on with your work. I'll come round and look at everyone's books in turn. You're first. What page are you doing?
BILL	This one.
MRS COLLINS	This is very messy. Look at this dirty smudge. And this one. And the edge of your book looks as if it's been *chewed*.

9

BILL	But I'm doing my best. And it's a lot better than what I did yesterday. Or the day before. In fact, it's a really good page – for me.
MRS COLLINS	Well it's not good enough for *me*. Now what about yours, Philip?
PHILIP	I'm doing this page.
MRS COLLINS	Not bad at all, Philip. Keep up the good work.
BILL	Let me see that, Philip.
PHILIP	Here you are.
BILL	But that's awful. That's disgusting. It's much, much worse than mine!
FLORA	Philip's letters are all wobbly.
TALILAH	They're straggling all over the page like camels lost in the desert.
BILL	It's much, much worse than mine. And she didn't say anything nice to me.
TALILAH	Or me.
FLORA	Or me.
PHILIP	Well, girls are *supposed* to be neater, aren't they?
ALL THE GIRLS	Why?
PHILIP	I don't know. They just *are*.

Scene 4: In the classroom (continued)

(BILL, MRS COLLINS, NICK, TALILAH, FLORA, PHILIP, KIRSTY and the WHOLE CLASS)

MRS COLLINS	It's time for group reading. What page are we on?
WHOLE CLASS	Page-for-ty-se-ven-Mis-sus-Col-lins.
MRS COLLINS	Page forty-seven. Ah, yes. The story of *Rapunzel*. What a nice old fairy tale that is. And it's table five's turn to take the main parts today. So you be the farmer, Nick.
NICK	Yes, Mrs Collins.
MRS COLLINS	You be the farmer's wife, Talilah.
TALILAH	Goody!
MRS COLLINS	You be the witch, Flora.
FLORA	Oh, great!
MRS COLLINS	You be the handsome prince, Philip.
PHILIP	Yes, well, I am rather handsome.
WHOLE CLASS	...groan...bleh...groan...bleh...
MRS COLLINS	Kirsty, you be the narrator. And who does that leave?
BILL	Me.
MRS COLLINS	Right then, dear. You get to be The Lovely Rapunzel.

11

BILL	*Me?*
MRS COLLINS	Why not? It's almost as if you're dressed for the part.
BILL	I don't believe this. I do not believe this!
MRS COLLINS	Right. Everyone happy?
KIRSTY	I am. I get to say the most.
FLORA	I get to say quite a bit.
TALILAH	I do, too.
NICK	So do I.
PHILIP	And me.
BILL	I hardly get to say *anything*.
KIRSTY	You get stolen by the witch.
TALILAH	And you get hidden at the top of a tower.
NICK	And you stay there for fifteen years.
PHILIP	And your hair grows very long.
FLORA	Very long indeed.
BILL	But I don't *do* anything. I just say '*Oooooooooh.*'
KIRSTY	That's a very good part.
WHOLE CLASS	'*Oooooooooh.*'
BILL	No it isn't. Mrs Collins, why doesn't Rapunzel have a better part?
MRS COLLINS	What do you mean?

BILL	Well, what I mean is, it's her story, isn't it? It's called *Rapunzel*. So how come she doesn't actually *do* anything?
MRS COLLINS	I don't know what you mean.
BILL	I mean, she didn't have to just sit there quietly growing her hair, did she? And nobody forced her to just sit on her bottom for fifteen years, waiting for a prince to come along and rescue her.
KIRSTY	That's right. She could have shown a bit of spirit.
TALILAH	Planned her own escape.
PHILIP	Cut off all her lovely long hair herself.
NICK	Braided it into a rope.
FLORA	Slid down it all by herself.
KIRSTY	And run home.
NICK	And she'd have been a lot more worth rescuing.
PHILIP	In fact, I don't think a handsome prince like myself would want to marry a big wimp like her.
MRS COLLINS	I don't know what's going on today. I really don't. One of you gets in a funny mood, and suddenly the whole lot of you are in a funny mood. Shall we read *Polly the Ace Pilot* instead?
WHOLE CLASS	Yes! Let's read that instead!

13

Scene 5: The Art Class

(MRS BANDA, BILL, LEILA, MELISSA, PAUL, WAYNE and the WHOLE CLASS)

MRS BANDA	Time for the art lesson. What's left in the cupboard?
LEILA	Not much.
MRS BANDA	Any coloured chalks?
PAUL	No. They're all gone.
MRS BANDA	Pastels, then?
LEILA	They're still damp from the roof leak.
MRS BANDA	Any clay?
PAUL	It's all dried up.
MRS BANDA	There *must* be crayons.
LEILA	The infants came and borrowed them last week, and they haven't brought them back yet.
MRS BANDA	So it's paints again, as usual. What colours do we have left in the tubs?
WAYNE	Pink.
MRS BANDA	And what's in that one?
MELISSA	Pink.
MRS BANDA	And in that one?
WAYNE	More pink.
MRS BANDA	And that one?

MELISSA	Pink again.
WAYNE	There's more pink here.
MRS BANDA	I've found some blue – no, I haven't. It's all gone.
MELISSA	Here's another pink.
WAYNE	This is pink, too.
MRS BANDA	Pink, pink! Nothing but pink!
WAYNE	What can you do with pink?
WHOLE CLASS	Nothing.
WAYNE	You can't paint pink dogs.
MELISSA	Or pink space vehicles.
WAYNE	Or pink trees.
MELISSA	Or pink battlefields.
MRS BANDA	There must be *something* that's all pink.
	(*First one person's eye falls on Bill. Then another's. Then another's. The silence grows. In the end, everyone is looking at Bill*)
BILL	Oh, no. Oh, no, no, no. Oh, no, no, no, no, no. Not me. Absolutely not. You can't. Oh, no, no, no, no, no.
MRS BANDA	Yes. Pink frock. Pink freckles. And now, pink, pink cheeks. Yes, you'll do beautifully. You're all pink. Now sit down in the middle where everyone can see you.

BILL	There's a curse on me today. A pink curse!
MRS BANDA	And don't *scowl,* dear, or you'll ruin their paintings!
BILL	Grrrrrrrrr.....

Scene 6: On the way to the school office

(MRS COLLINS, BILL, SCHOOL NURSE, HEADMASTER, SCHOOL JANITOR and SCHOOL SECRETARY)

MRS COLLINS Now, while everyone clears up their desk, I'd like you to do a little job for me. Take this key along to the office.

BILL Righty-ho.

(*Then he meets the school nurse.*)

NURSE Are you going along to the office with that key?

BILL Yes.

NURSE Oh, good. You can save me a journey. Would you take all these medical forms along for me? And whatever you do, don't drop them or you'll get them all mixed up.

BILL Righty-ho.

(*Then he meets the headmaster.*)

HEADMASTER You look very sensible and responsible. Are you going along to the office with all those medical forms and that key?

BILL Yes.

HEADMASTER Good. Take all these little bottles of coloured ink along for me, will you? Mind you don't spill them down your sweet little frock.

BILL	(*through clenched teeth*) Righty-ho.
	(*Then Bill meets the janitor.*)
JANITOR	I see that you're going along to the office with all those medical forms and that key and those little bottles of paint. Will you take all these spare tennis balls along for me, please?
BILL	Righty-ho.
	(*Bill shuffles off down the corridor.*)
JANITOR	Mind you don't drop everything!
BILL	Has everyone gone? Am I alone at last? Good. Now I can slip into the boys' toilets in this stupid pink frock without anyone pointing and laughing. I'll just shove all this stuff away in my pockets. Pockets . . . Pockets . . . Oh, no! This stupid frock doesn't have any pockets! It has frills. It has pleats. It has bows. It even has fancy buttons. But it doesn't have any pockets! How is a normal human being supposed to live without pockets? Go on! Answer me that! How is a normal human being who leads a normal human life supposed to live without having any pockets????
SECRETARY	Who is that out in the corridor doing all that yelling? Come in here at once.
BILL	I'll have to push the door open with my foot. Oh, no. I'm in trouble. The tennis balls are rolling. The key's sliding. The

little bottles of coloured ink are falling off.
The medical forms are going – Oh!

(*He drops the lot.*)

JANITOR

HEADMASTER

NURSE   (*all appearing*) Now that wasn't very
               sensible, was it?

MRS COLLINS

SECRETARY

BILL   It wasn't nearly as stupid as making a dress
               without pockets!

Scene 7: A wet break in the classroom

(ROHAN, BILL, MRS COLLINS, MELISSA, MARTIN, PHILIP, TALILAH, WAYNE and the WHOLE CLASS)

TALILAH	It's pouring with rain.
PHILIP	We can't go outside.
WAYNE	Mrs Collins, can we get out the comic box?
MRS COLLINS	I'll give them out so we don't have a riot. There. One for you. And one for you. And one for you ... (*lastly, to Bill*) ... and one for you.
BILL	But this is a *Mandy*.
MRS COLLINS	Would you prefer a *June*? Or a *Judy*?
BILL	Can't I have a *Beano*? Or a *Dandy*? Or a *Hotspur*? Or a *Lion*? Or a *Victor*?
MRS COLLINS	I'm sorry. They've all gone. Here's a *Bunty*, with almost no pages missing.
BILL	I don't want a *Bunty*. Hey, Melissa. Is that a *Beano* you're reading? Will you swap? This is a *Bunty* with almost no pages missing.
MELISSA	You have to be joking!
BILL	Hey, Flora! Flora! Would you like a *Bunty*?

FLORA	No, thank you. I've got a *Dandy* here.
BILL	Rohan! Rohan, I'll swap you my practically brand new comic here for that tatty old *Valiant* you're reading.
ROHAN	What have you got? Is it a *Hotspur?*
BILL	No. It's a *Bunty.*
ROHAN	Ha, ha, ha. Very funny. No thank you.
BILL	Hey, Martin. Will you swap with me as soon as you've finished that *Victor?*
MARTIN	Sure. What have you got there?
BILL	(*very, very softly*) A *Bunty.*
MARTIN	What? I can't hear you.
BILL	(*very softly*) A *Bunty.*
MARTIN	I still can't hear you.
BILL	(*softly*) A *Bunty.*
MARTIN	Say it again, louder.
BILL	(*yelling*) It's a *Bunty*!!! OK??? A *Bunty*!!!!
MARTIN	No thanks.
MRS COLLINS	Be quiet, you two, please. And get on with your reading.
BILL	Oh, all right. Hey. This story isn't so bad ...
MARTIN	What story?

BILL	Well, you see, there's this really brave orphan girl called Leila who has to lead her lame pony through a dangerous war zone, and there are bombs dropping all around them and –
MELISSA	Are you ready to swap now?
BILL	What?
MELISSA	I've finished this one now. So do you want to swap?
BILL	Can I just finish this really exciting story first?
MELISSA	No. It's now or never.
BILL	Oh, all right. Here you are.
	(*He's contentedly reading his Beano when Rohan comes up.*)
ROHAN	Here. You take this one and I'll have that one.
BILL	What *is* that?
ROHAN	It's a *June*.
BILL	No, thanks.
ROHAN	Come on. Don't be mean. Swap comics with me. I don't want this one.
BILL	I don't want it either. I'm busy reading this.
ROHAN	Give it over.
BILL	Why should I?

ROHAN	Because this one's soppy. Someone in a frilly pink frock might want to read it. But I don't.
BILL	Neither do I!
ROHAN	I bet you do really.
BILL	No, I don't! Let go! You'll tear my comic. Let go! Let go of it, or I'll bash you!
ROHAN	I'll bash you back!
BILL	Right!
ROHAN	Right!
BILL	Ouch!
ROHAN	Ouch!
BILL	Let go my hair!
ROHAN	Let go my ears!
WHOLE CLASS	Mrs Collins! Mrs Collins! They're fighting!
MRS COLLINS	How dare you? How *dare* you! What *is* going on? Who started this fight?
ROHAN	It wasn't *my* fault.
BILL	*I* didn't start it. *You* did.
ROHAN	No, *you* did!
MRS COLLINS	Oh, yes? Is that likely, Rohan? Do you expect me to believe that someone in a pretty pink frock covered with frills is going to pick a fight with someone like you, wearing great heavy shoes?

BILL   Saved by a frock!

MRS COLLINS   No, you're not! I'm punishing both of you.
                   Now you sit down here, Rohan. And you
                   sit down over here. And both of you can
                   write 'Fighting is stupid and fighting is
                   ugly' ten times, in your best writing.

                   (*They sit side by side, writing, both
                   scowling horribly.*)

MELISSA   (*whispering to Rohan*) You look so *angry*,
                   Rohan!

FLORA   (*whispering to Bill*) And you look so *upset!*

Scene 8: Afternoon races

(BILL, MRS COLLINS, PAUL, ASTRID, TALILAH, KIRSTY, LAURA, MARK and the WHOLE CLASS)

MRS COLLINS	Races! First race!
ROHAN	People in pretty pink frocks against people not in pretty pink frocks.
BILL	That's not fair. That's me against everyone else.
ASTRID	People wearing red against people not wearing red.
WHOLE CLASS	Puff, puff, puff, puff, puff, puff – hooray!
LAURA	People who use plastic bags against people who still use real dustbins.
WHOLE CLASS	Puff, puff, puff, puff, puff, puff – hooray!
BILL	This stupid pink frock keeps flapping up and showing my underpants. I try and hold it down, but then I can't run fast.
MRS COLLINS	Do stop fiddling with your frock, dear. You're getting grubby fingerprints all round the hem.
BILL	I can't help it. The stupid thing keeps flapping up round my waist. No wonder most of the girls don't bother to wear things like this.
MRS COLLINS	Next race?
MARK	People with dark hair against people with light hair.

25

WHOLE CLASS	Puff, puff, puff, puff, puff, puff – hooray!
MRS COLLINS	Next?
ROHAN	People who like reading against people who don't like reading.
WHOLE CLASS	Puff, puff, puff, puff, puff, puff – hooray!
MRS COLLINS	You all divide into groups of five for the big last race while I go off and get a glass of water.
BILL	Are you in the same group as me, Talilah?
TALILAH	Yes, I am. And so are Kirsty and Astrid and Paul.
KIRSTY	Paul just told me he's never won a race, not ever.
ASTRID	That's because he wasn't well for a long time when he was a baby.
TALILAH	He just can't run very well.
ASTRID	Fancy never, ever having won a race! I've won *thousands*.
KIRSTY	We could fix it so he won this one. Just this once.
TALILAH	What? Arrange it so everyone else falls over?
ASTRID	I *never* fall over.
TALILAH	You could pretend to get stitch, then.

ASTRID	Yes. I could do that. Owwwwwww! Oooooooh! Yeeeeowwww!
KIRSTY	Don't practise now. He'll guess. Ssssh!
BILL	Why are you all whispering? What are you hiding from me and Paul?
KIRSTY	We're not hiding anything from you. We're hiding it from Paul.
BILL	What?
KIRSTY	We're going to let him win the race.
BILL	How? Paul never wins races.
ASTRID	Well, he's going to win this one! I'm going to get stitch. Kirsty and Talilah can bump into one another. And you can trip over your own feet.
BILL	I *never* trip over my own feet.
ASTRID	There's always a first time for everything. And it's today.
BILL	Put you together for three minutes and you're whispering and fixing up secrets.
ASTRID	That's just the way we are. Now don't spoil this. Remember. Paul's going to win our race.
BILL	All right. If you say so.
MRS COLLINS	Right! I'm back! Which is the first group?

ASTRID KIRSTY BILL TALILAH PAUL	We are!
KIRSTY	Come along, Paul. Get in your place.
PAUL	I don't know why I even bother. I never win.
TALILAH	You never know...
MRS COLLINS	Is everyone ready? On your marks...
ASTRID	(*in a whisper*) Bad luck, then, you three!
MRS COLLINS	Get set! Go!
WHOLE CLASS	Off they go! Come on, Talilah! Run, Kirsty! Hurry up, Paul! Good old Astrid! In front as usual! Oh!
ASTRID	Oh! I've got stitch. Oooooh! Aaaaagh! Yeeeouch!
WHOLE CLASS	Now Kirsty and Talilah are out in front.
KIRSTY	Get out of my way, Talilah!
TALILAH	Get out of my way, Kirsty!
KIRSTY TALILAH	Whooops!
WHOLE CLASS	Look who's in front now!

28

BILL	It's me! It's me! I'm winning!
ASTRID	(*hissing*) Time to trip over your feet!
BILL	I'm nearly there!
TALILAH	(*hissing*) Trip over your feet! Quick!
BILL	I've almost won!
KIRSTY	(*hissing*) If you don't trip over your feet this second, you're going to wi–
BILL	I've won! I've won! I've won!
ASTRID	(*sarcastically*) Oh, brilliant!
TALILAH	(*sarcastically*) Amazing!
KIRSTY	(*sarcastically*) Wonderful!
ASTRID	Isn't it funny, how all some people can think of is themselves, and winning, winning, winning?
BILL	That's just the way I am. I can't help it. I've won! I've won! I've won!
PAUL	And I'm second! I'm second! I'm second! I've never, ever been runner-up before!
ASTRID	Well, that's something, I suppose.
PAUL	*Something*? It's brilliant! Amazing! Wonderful!
BILL	See! Everything turned out fine.

Scene 9: Going home

(BILL, MRS COLLINS, MUM, MALCOLM and the WHOLE CLASS)

(The bell rings.)

MRS COLLINS   Right. Off you go.

WHOLE CLASS   Hooray!

MRS COLLINS   *(to Bill)* Not you, dear. I'd like a little word with you before you rush off home.

BILL   What have I done?

MRS COLLINS   Nothing. Nothing. It's just – oh, I don't know. There's something different about you today. I can't think what, but there's something really strange about you. You're not quite *yourself*, you know.

BILL   Oh, I know. I know.

MRS COLLINS   Well. Off you go. I just hope that you're your old self again tomorrow.

BILL   Oh, so do I! So do I!

MRS COLLINS   Goodbye, then.

BILL   Bye. She's right. I'm not myself today. But how can a silly pink frock with fancy shell buttons have made such a difference – to every single thing that happened? All day long! Well, never mind. At least the day's nearly over. I'm going home now. I've had quite enough. In fact, if one more thing happens to me today… One more thing . . . Well, people had better watch out, that's all I can say.

MALCOLM   (*wolf-whistling*)   Wheeeeet-whoooooo!

BILL   What was that?

MALCOLM   (*wolf-whistling*) Wheeeet-whooooo!

BILL   Who are you whistling at? Are you whistling at me?

MALCOLM   Nice pretty frock . . .

BILL   Because what I'm wearing is none of your business.

MALCOLM   Can't you even take a joke?

BILL   No. No, I can't take a joke. I've had enough. And I won't be whistled at, either. Whistling is for dogs. And I am not a dog. I am – I am –

What am I?
I am a *person*, that is what I am.
So take that! And that!

MALCOLM   Watch out! You'll have me over in the dustbins!

BILL   I don't care.

MALCOLM   Careful! I'm falling!

BILL   Good!

MALCOLM   Stop thumping me! Help! Help!

BILL   And one for luck! There!

MALCOLM	Look at me! I'm covered in carrot peelings and tea leaves!
BILL	Well, that'll teach you a lesson, won't it? In future, whistle at dogs, not at people!
MUM	Good heavens!
BILL	Mum!
MUM	I don't believe this! What *do* you look like?
BILL	I don't know. What do I look like?
MUM	You look *disgusting*. Look at this pretty pink frock. It's *ruined*.
BILL	What's wrong with it?
MUM	What's wrong with it? I'll tell you what's wrong with it. It looks as if you've been trying to play football in it.
BILL	Well, I have.
MUM	And it looks as if people have been painting with pink poster paints all around you.
BILL	Well, they have.
MUM	And it looks as if you've been carrying little bottles of coloured ink close to your chest.
BILL	Well, I have.
MUM	And it looks as if you've been in a fight in it.

BILL	Well, I have.
MUM	And it looks as if you've been running races in it.
BILL	Well, I have.
MUM	And it looks as if you've been putting your grubby fingers all over the hem, to try and keep it down.
BILL	Well, I have.
MUM	And it looks as if you've been on top of the dustbins in it.
BILL	Well, I have.
MUM	Well, you can just take it off!
BILL	Can I? Can I?
MUM	Come on. Take it off at once.
BILL	I'll take the frock off, but it won't end the nightmare... Wait a minute! I'm wrong! The nightmare *has* ended. Am I sure?
	(*Bill turns his back discreetly.*)
	Yes, I'm sure!
	(*He turns round to face the world again.*)
	I am a boy again! Hooray! I am a boy again!
MUM	Filthy! It's absolutely filthy! And it's torn. I warn you, this is the very last time I ever send you to school in a frock!

BILL	(*on his knees*) Oh, do you promise, Mum? Do you *promise*?
MUM	Yes, I most certainly do! You'll never, ever go to school in a frock again!
BILL	And I never did!
WHOLE CLASS	And he never did!

Drama activities

1 Work in groups of four. Each group should choose three important moments in the play which best sum up what happens to Bill during his day at school.

As a group, set up three still pictures (like 'freeze-frames' on a video) of the moments you have chosen. Practise going from one still picture to another as smoothly as possible and remember to show each character's attitude to Bill.

For example, to start with, you may choose the moment when Bill arrives in the school playground. You could then include other children, teachers, and perhaps the headmaster in the picture.

Prepare your pictures for about 15 minutes, and then each group shows their three freeze-frames to the rest of the class.

You can develop this idea by making up other sets of freeze-frames to show important moments in the play.

2 Working in small groups, choose a short scene from the play. Here are some possibilities:

- Bill gets up and goes to school.
- Football in the playground.
- The art lesson.
- The comic box at lunch-time.
- The races.
- Bill's journey home.

Reread the scene you have chosen carefully, looking for sound effects, the characters involved and the atmosphere of the scene. Next, rehearse the scene and, either read it to the class, or make a tape recording of it.

You can extend this by inventing and scripting your own short scene based on an imaginary incident in another school.

Writing and talking about the play

1 For the first few lines of this play, Bill is the narrator. He talks directly to you and tells you what is happening. Then it changes, and from then on, Bill is either talking directly to the other characters or to himself.

Take the section of the play from the start to where Mum goes to work, and re-write it so Bill continues to tell the story, just as he does in the first few lines. Or you could re-write it with Mum as narrator telling what happens from her point of view.

This is a good opportunity to look at the differences between the indirect speech of a narrator and setting out direct speech in stories.

2 What do you think that Bill learns during the course of the day when he wears the frock? Discuss this with one or more people and make some notes. On your own, choose a magazine (or newspaper or comic) and write a letter to the problem page as if you were Bill, describing your experiences and explaining what it is that you have learnt.

3 In a small group, or a whole class group, discuss what Bill gained and what he lost from the experience of being treated like a girl. Try to relate this to your own experiences of being female or of being male. What do you like and what do you not like about the way you are treated? What do you like or not like about the ways in which you are expected to behave?

4 'I might have known that the day was going to be a nightmare . . . ' Discuss with one or more people some of the nightmarish things that happen to Bill in the play.

- Either write a play about a girl who wakes up one morning and finds that she is being treated like a boy.

- Or write a story about your own nightmare. The essential elements of the story should be: you wake up and you are different in some way; you are treated differently by the people you know; you learn from the experience.

PUBLISHED BY BBC EDUCATIONAL PUBLISHING AND
LONGMAN GROUP UK LIMITED

BBC Educational Publishing
a division of
BBC Enterprises Limited
Woodlands
80 Wood Lane
London W12 0TT

Addison Wesley Longman Limited,
Edinburgh Gate, Harlow,
Essex CM20 2JE,
England, and Associated
Companies throughout the
World

Original text by Anne Fine © 1989 published by Methuen Childrens Books

Play script Anne Fine © 1992

This educational edition © BBC Enterprises Limited/Longman Group
UK Limited 1992

This educational edition first published 1992
Tenth impression 1998

ISBN 0 582 09556 5

Cover illustration by Mike Sharpe
Printed in Malaysia, GPS